This Little Tiger book belongs to:

_____

_____

Especially for baby Edith, with love
~ M C B

For Harriet James
~ T M

LITTLE TIGER
An imprint of Little Tiger Press Limited
1 Coda Studios, 189 Munster Road, London SW6 6AW
Imported into the EEA by Penguin Random House Ireland,
Morrison Chambers, 32 Nassau Street, Dublin D02 YH68
www.littletiger.co.uk

First published in Great Britain 2019
This edition published 2020
Text copyright © M Christina Butler 2019
Illustrations copyright © Tina Macnaughton 2019

M Christina Butler and Tina Macnaughton have asserted
their rights to be identified as the author and illustrator of this
work under the Copyright, Designs and Patents Act, 1988

A CIP catalogue record for this book is available from the British Library
All rights reserved • ISBN 978-1-78881-385-3
Printed in China • LTP/1400/5168/0523
10 9 8 7 6 5 4

One Christmas Journey

M Christina Butler • Tina Macnaughton

LITTLE TIGER
LONDON

Little Hedgehog and his friends were out walking in the snow, gathering holly for their Christmas party.

"Goodness! What's that?" exclaimed Fox as a strange figure wobbled towards them.

"Is it a present on legs?" cried Rabbit.

"No," chuckled Little Hedgehog.

"I think it's Squirrel!"

"Wherever are you going with all those bags?"
asked Little Hedgehog, rushing up to help.
  "Hello," gasped Squirrel. "I'm taking
Christmas presents and snacks to
Grandpa Squirrel. He's got a
terrible cold and can't get
out in all this snow."

"We'll help you!" offered Little Hedgehog.
"Come on, everyone!"
"Oh, thank you!" beamed Squirrel as
he shared out the parcels.

The friends followed Squirrel up, up, up
the steep snowy path to Grandpa Squirrel's
house on Rocky Ridge.

"We're here!" cheered the baby mice at last.

"Oh my!" declared Grandpa Squirrel, opening
his door. "Come in! What a lovely surprise!
I'll make some cocoa to warm you up."

As they shared stories and nibbled cookies, Little Hedgehog noticed fresh flakes of snow falling outside.

"We'd better get going," he said.

"Thanks for all your help!" exclaimed Squirrel.

"And take care," warned Grandpa Squirrel. "The path can get very slippery."

In a flurry of snowflakes
the friends made their way
carefully down the icy path.
"Steady, everyone," cried Badger.
But it was too late . . .

Whoosh!

Little Hedgehog slipped.

"Look out!" he called.

But then Fox skidded into Badger, who bumped into Rabbit and all the mice! Soon everyone was slip-sliding down the path.

Thud! They landed in a
higgledy-piggledy heap.

"Is everyone all right?"
spluttered Little Hedgehog.

"We're fine!" squeaked Mouse.

"So are we!" added Fox and Badger.

"That just leaves . . ."

"Rabbit!" they all called. "Where
are you, Rabbit?"

And their cry echoed
round the mountains.

"Here I am!" answered Rabbit from under a snowy drift. "But what's that rumbling sound?"

They looked at each other as the snow began to shudder and shake.

"AVALANCHE!" yelled Badger. "Everyone into this cave! Quick!"

Swoosh!

Safely inside, the friends peered out as
a rush of snow swept past the cave.
"That was close!" said Fox. All at once
the snow stopped and everything was still.

"The snow is covering the path!" squeaked
Mouse as they stepped outside.

"We're stuck!" cried Rabbit. "We'll miss
Christmas!"

"There must be another way home," said
Badger. "I think we can scramble down
round the rocks."

"But it'll be dark soon," shivered a baby mouse. "We might get lost!"

"I know what to do!" said Little Hedgehog, unravelling his hat. "We'll use this wool to tie ourselves together. That way we won't get separated as we climb down!"

Little Hedgehog fastened one end of the wool to a tree trunk. Then everyone wrapped the yarn around their waists.

"Take your time, and be careful!" warned Badger as they began to edge their way down the hillside.

"We're nearly there!" called Little Hedgehog,
leading the way. But the wool was wet
and slippery between his paws.
"Eek!" he cried, starting to slide.
"The wool's running out!"
Down,

down,

down, he slipped . . .

. . .until a bright red pom-pom
stopped his fall!

"I'm OK!" he shouted.
"I've been saved by my
bobble!"

"Hooray!" everyone
cheered, jumping safely
to the ground.

"What an adventure!" said Little Hedgehog
as the friends walked up to Badger's house.
"But look at my poor hat . . ."

"Don't worry," smiled Badger kindly.
"We can fix that!"

And that's just what they did!

With Christmas cupcakes and mugs of cocoa, Badger showed Little Hedgehog how to knit his hat back together.

"My favourite hat will be as good as new!" smiled Little Hedgehog. "Thank you, Badger! And Happy Christmas, everyone!"